Brothers Grimm
fairy tales

Illustrated By
Greg Hildebrandt

The Unicorn Publishing House, Inc.
New Jersey

Snow-White and the Seven Dwarfs

Once upon a time there was a beautiful but wicked Queen. She had a magic mirror, and she would stand before it and say, "Mirror, mirror on the wall,/Who is the fairest of them all?" And the mirror would answer, "You are fairest of them all." But one day when the Queen asked, the mirror said:

"Queen, you are full fair, 'tis true,/But young Snow-White is fairer than you." Snow-White was her step-daughter, and had now grown into a beautiful and gentle young woman.

The Queen was furious. From that moment on her heart turned to hatred against Snow-White. She called for a huntsmen, and told him to take Snow-White into the woods and put her to death.

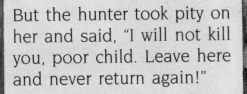

But the hunter took pity on her and said, "I will not kill you, poor child. Leave here and never return again!"

Snow-White fled deep into the wild woods. She was in terror at every turn, but she didn't not know what to do except to go deeper and deeper into the forest. In the heart of the wood she came upon a tiny cottage.

Tired and hungry, she decided to go inside to rest. She found no one was at home, so she helped herself to a bit of bread and drink, and then laid down on a tiny bed and soon fell fast asleep.

It was quite dark when the little men came home. They were seven dwarfs who dug for gold in the mountains. Finding Snow-White asleep, they decided to let the poor child rest until morning.

When Snow-White awoke, she was greeted warmly by the little men. She told them about the wicked Queen and how she had tried to kill her. They decided she should stay with them, but they warned:

"Beware of your stepmother! Let no one into the house." Snow-White thanked her new friends, and the seven dwarfs set off for a good day's work.

Thinking Snow-White dead, the Queen vainly stepped up to her mirror, and said, "Mirror, mirror, on the wall,/Who is the fairest of them all?"

And the mirror said, "Queen, you are a beauty rare,/But Snow-White living in the glen/With the seven little men/Is a thousand times more fair."

The Queen tore at her hair, crying, "No! She lives! She lives!" After a time, she said, "I shall kill her myself! By black arts I will undo this child!" And with witchcraft she made a poison apple.

She dressed as an old beggar woman and went to the dwarfs' house. She called, "My dear, I was passing by and heard your sweet singing. I have picked some sweet apples, won't you have one?"

No sooner did Snow-White bite into the apple, than she fell as if dead. But she was not dead.

The apple didn't kill her, but put her into a deep sleep from which nothing the dwarfs did would wake her. In sorrow, the dwarfs placed her in a glass case, that they could watch over her as they prayed and waited. Then one day, a prince rode by.

The young prince fell in love at once with the sleeping maiden. He begged the dwarfs but one little kiss from her sweet lips. Bending down, he gently kissed Snow-White, and the evil spell was broken. She awoke, smiling.

He asked her hand in marriage and Snow-White accepted. He took her away to his kingdom. As for the Queen, she stood in front of her mirror, crying. She grew old, died, and fell to dust.

The Elves and the Shoemaker

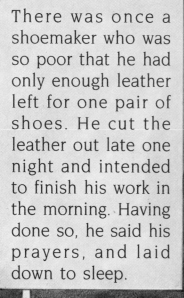

There was once a shoemaker who was so poor that he had only enough leather left for one pair of shoes. He cut the leather out late one night and intended to finish his work in the morning. Having done so, he said his prayers, and laid down to sleep.

In the morning, when he awoke, he was amazed to find a finished pair of shoes on his table. He called to his wife, saying, "How can this be? I but cut the leather out last night. And look at them. Whoever made these is a master craftsman, of that I have no doubt."

At that moment a man came in, who wanted to purchase a pair of shoes. "Oh, my yes, these are simply perfect! Simply perfect! Here you are," he cried, and he gave the shoemaker enough money to buy leather for *two* pairs of shoes!

He was going to make the shoes the next day, but again when he awoke he found the shoes had already been made.

And he had no lack of customers. From that time on, the shoemaker would cut the leather at night and awake to finished shoes in the morning. Before long, he was quite wealthy.

Now one evening, just before Christmas, he said to his wife, "Why don't we stay up late and hide to see who is giving us all this help." They hid in a corner of the room and waited. At midnight there came two little men through the window.

They were naked, except for tiny green leaves around their waists. They stopped to look and listen, and then they jumped on the table.

They went to work at once, and began to stitch, sew, and hammer the shoes together so quickly that the shoemaker could not believe his eyes! Then they ran swiftly away.

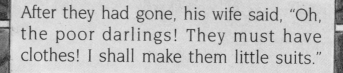

After they had gone, his wife said, "Oh, the poor darlings! They must have clothes! I shall make them little suits."

From leather she made them each a little cap, suit, and shoes. When they came the next night they found the charming clothes, and cried with joy. Quick as could be, they put them on.

Then, dressed in their pretty clothes, they danced, and sang, "Now we're boys so fine and neat,/Why make shoes for other's feet!" And they jumped out the window. They never came back again, but the shoemaker gave thanks every night for all they had done.

The Frog Prince

Long ago there was a King's daughter, a beautiful child, who loved to play with her ball down by a pond. Now it happened one day that the ball fell in the water and sank to the bottom.

She began to weep, for she could never reach it herself. Then she heard a voice, saying, "Why do you weep, my Princess?" It was an ugly Frog.

"I weep because my golden ball has fallen into the pond and I cannot reach it," she said.
"Oh, do not cry," said the Frog. "I can get your ball. What will the King's daughter give me if I do?"
"Anything you wish, dear Frog."

"If you will love me and be my playmate, let me eat from your plate and drink from your cup, and let me sleep in your bed—I shall get your ball." The Princess promised, and the Frog went down for her ball.

The Frog came up again with the ball in his mouth. The Princess took it and started off for the castle. "Wait! Wait! I cannot hop that fast!" But the Princess ran away.

That night a knock came at the castle door, and a voice could be heard, saying. "You promised me, Princess. Now come and let me in!"
Going to the door, she found the Frog waiting outside.
"Go away, you *horrid* Frog!"

But her father, the King, called out to his daughter, saying, "Come here, my child, and tell me what this is all about. Who is at the door?"

And the Princess told her father how she had lost her ball, and that she promised a Frog she would be his friend and companion if he would only swim down and get it for her.

"That which you promise you *must* keep," said the King. "Go, and let the Frog in."

She did as her father commanded, and the Frog followed her to the dining room. "Lift me up," said the Frog, "that I may sit with you."

"Now move your golden plate near me, that I may eat with you." She did so, but turned away in disgust to see him eat. The Frog, however, ate heartily and took no notice.

"I have had enough," the Frog finally said. "Come, take me up to your room, for I am tired and need to go to sleep." At this, she began to weep.

The King became angry at the sight of the Princess crying, and said once more: "What you promised in your time of need, you *must* now fulfill. The highest price of anything must always be one's word."

She dried her tears, and picked the Frog up with her finger and thumb, and carried him to her room. Once there, she placed him on the floor.

"I am as tired as you. Pick me up and place me on your little bed that I may sleep. If you don't, I shall tell your father you can't keep a promise." She began to weep softly once again, but she started to do as the Frog asked.

The Frog, seeing she would keep her word, said, "My princess, you do not have to place me on your clean bed. You have kept your word to me. And I am *not* what I seem to be."

And suddenly the Frog turned into a handsome and noble Prince. "Forgive me, Princess, for this poor trick. From first I saw you, I fell in love. But I had to know if you could be true to your word in both heart and deed. I had a wizard transform me into the Frog. I wish your hand in marriage, if you'll have me, and I promise no tricks."

The Princess accepted, and they were married soon after. And the Prince was as true to his word as the Princess was, and together, they lived a very long and happy life.

hansel and Gretel

Deep in a forest there lived a woodcutter with his wife and two children. He named his son Hansel and his daughter Gretel. There had been a famine in the land, and he no longer had any food to feed his family. One night, his wife said, "Tomorrow, we will take the children far into the forest, give them some bread, and leave them there."

"Leave *my* children! How could I? I won't!" he cried. "You *will*, husband, or we shall all starve! They will find a kinder death in the forest!"

Now Hansel and Gretel were still awake and heard the terrible fate awaiting them in the morning. But Hansel had a plan. He told Gretel: "Don't worry, for as father takes us into the forest, I will drop crumbs of bread along the way. We can return back home by following the crumbs along the path after they've gone. Why, I bet we can be back home before they are!"

In the morning, the wife woke them, saying, "Here, children, take this bread for your supper today. We must go deep into the forest to gather good wood and we want you to come along with us. Hurry now, we have a long way to go before the day is done." And the family set off into the deep woods.

As they walked along, Hansel would drop a crumb of bread behind him from time to time when he was sure his father wasn't watching. They walked all day into the deep, deep wood.

Evening finally came, and their father said they should stop. He wanted so to bring his children back home with him, but he knew his wife would not stand for it. He said sadly, "Children, I have to go farther off to gather wood. I will make you a nice fire, and you can stay here." And with a tear, he left the children alone.

Later that evening, the children set off along the path, following the bread crumbs that Hansel had thrown down. But they hadn't gone far when the bread crumbs just disappeared. Sadly, during the day a thousand birds had swooped down to feed on the bread. They were now lost in the dark forest. Not knowing where to go, they decided to lay down and sleep for the night.

In the morning, they began walking to try to find a way out. Deep in the wood, they came upon a cottage—and the roof was made of gingerbread!

Hansel and Gretel could hardly believe their eyes! They ran to the house, for they hadn't eaten in two days, and began pulling great chunks of gingerbread from the roof.

No sooner were they stuffing their mouths full of tasty gingerbread, than a voice came from behind, saying, "Nibbling, nibbling like a mouse,/Who's that nibbling the gingerbread house?"
Looking up, the children saw an old woman at the door, and they both dropped their food in fright.

"Don't be frightened, children," she said. "Ah, my dears, what has brought you here. Come in, and I will feed you. Come in."

The old woman was *really* a wicked old Witch, and as soon as the children came inside she grabbed them up and threw them in a cage. "Now I have you, and you won't escape!" she said, and then with a wicked laugh, she thought, "What dainty morsels they will make!" For she planned on having them for dinner.

The Witch thought she would eat Gretel first, so she turned to Hansel, and said, "Mind your ways, boy, or I'll hurt your sister!" Then she had Gretel set the table while she lit the oven.

"Go, child, into the oven and fetch me that pan in the back," the Witch told her. "Be quick!"
"But I don't know how to get in?" Gretel cried.
"See here, it's easy!" And as the Witch bent down, Gretel pushed her in.

The Witch was dead. Gretel freed Hansel, and the two ran from the cottage and into the woods. After two days, they found their way home. Their father hugged them, and said, "Oh, forgive me, children! I promise never to send you away again. We will be together forever."

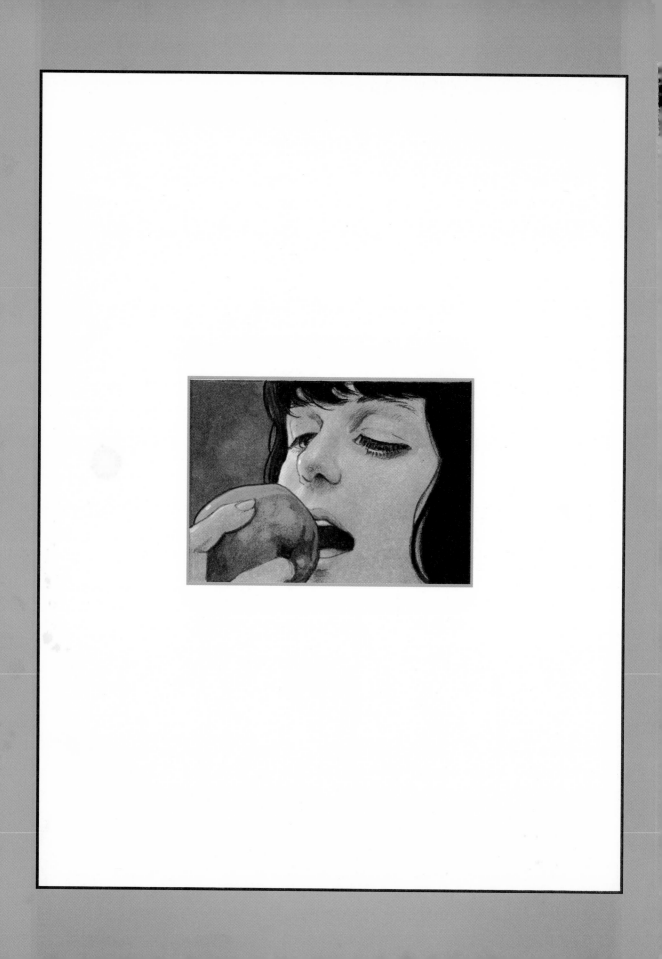